Advice & Wishes
for the
Bride-to-be

MARISSA

Advice for the **Bride-to-be**

♥♥♥♥♥♥♥♥♥♥♥♥♥♥

Dear <u>Marissa</u> (Bride's name)
I am so <u>fuzzy</u> that you are getting hitched! You
(Adjective)
and <u>zach</u> make such a <u>pink</u> couple. I <u>run</u>
(Groom's name)   (Adjective)   (verb)
all the way from <u>Portland</u> to celebrate with you
(place)
today. Without any doubt you will be the most <u>spicy</u>
(Adjective)
spouse because of your unique ability to <u>sleep</u>.
(verb)
As your friend of <u>8</u> years, I will leave you with
(number)
a little bit of wisdom. On your wedding day make
sure you <u>skip</u> and don't forget to <u>hop</u> !!! To keep
(verb)   (verb)
a happy marriage, never, ever fight about <u>bed</u>.
(noun)
<u>balloon</u> and <u>pillow</u> and tell each other <u>eye noodles alread</u>
(noun)   (noun)   (a phrase)
daily. I wish you lots of <u>truck</u> and <u>pizza</u>
(noun)   (noun)
for many years to come!

With Love, <u>marissa</u>
(your name)

♥♥♥♥♥♥♥♥♥♥♥♥♥♥

KATIE :)

Advice for the Bride-to-be

♥♥♥♥♥♥♥♥♥♥♥♥♥♥♥

Dear _____ (Bride's name)

I am so _slimcut_ that you are getting hitched! You
(Adjective)

and _Zach_ make such a _brown_ couple. I _ran_
(Groom's name)   (Adjective)   (verb)

all the way from _Nashvill_ to celebrate with you
(place)

today. Without any doubt you will be the most _creepy_
(Adjective)

spouse because of your unique ability to _pumping_
(verb)

As your friend of _7_ years, I will leave you with
(number)

a little bit of wisdom. On your wedding day make

sure you _fucked_ and don't forget to _felt_ !!! To keep
(verb)   (verb)

a happy marriage, never, ever fight about _boat_.
(noun)

pony and _____ and tell each other _fuck_
(noun)   (noun)   (a phrase)

daily. I wish you lots of _____ and _____
(noun)   (noun)

for many years to come!

With Love, _____
(your name)

♥♥♥♥♥♥♥♥♥♥♥♥♥♥♥

Advice for the Bride-to-be

♥ ♡ ♥ ♡ ♥ ♡ ♥ ♡ ♥ ♡ ♥ ♡ ♥

Dear _____ (Bride's name)

I am so _____ that you are getting hitched! You
            (Adjective)

and _____ make such a _____ couple. I _____
       (Groom's name)   (Adjective)   (verb)

all the way from _____ to celebrate with you
                          (place)

today. Without any doubt you will be the most _____
                                                    (Adjective)

spouse because of your unique ability to _____ .
                                               (verb)

As your friend of _____ years, I will leave you with
                      (number)

a little bit of wisdom. On your wedding day make

sure you _____ and don't forget to _____ !!! To keep
              (verb)   (verb)

a happy marriage, never, ever fight about _____ .
                                                (noun)

_____ and _____ and tell each other _____
 (noun)   (noun)   (a phrase)

daily. I wish you lots of _____ and _____
                               (noun)   (noun)

for many years to come!

With Love, _____

(your name)

♥ ♡ ♥ ♡ ♥ ♡ ♥ ♡ ♥ ♡ ♥ ♡ ♥

Advice for the Bride-to-be

♥♥♥♥♥♥♥♥♥♥♥♥♥

Dear _____ (Bride's name)

I am so _____ that you are getting hitched! You
(Adjective)

and _____ make such a _____ couple. I _____
(Groom's name)   (Adjective)   (verb)

all the way from _____ to celebrate with you
(place)

today. Without any doubt you will be the most _____
(Adjective)

spouse because of your unique ability to _____ .
(verb)

As your friend of ____ years, I will leave you with
(number)

a little bit of wisdom. On your wedding day make

sure you ____ and don't forget to ____ !!! To keep
(verb)   (verb)

a happy marriage, never, ever fight about _____ .
(noun)

_____ and _____ and tell each other _____
(noun)   (noun)   (a phrase)

daily. I wish you lots of _____ and _____
(noun)   (noun)

for many years to come!

With Love, _____
(your name)

Advice for the Bride-to-be

♥♥♥♥♥♥♥♥♥♥♥♥♥

Dear _____ (Bride's name)

I am so _____ that you are getting hitched! You
(Adjective)

and _____ make such a _____ couple. I _____
(Groom's name)   (Adjective)   (verb)

all the way from _____ to celebrate with you
(place)

today. Without any doubt you will be the most ____
(Adjectiv)

spouse because of your unique ability to _____.
(verb)

As your friend of _____ years, I will leave you with
(number)

a little bit of wisdom. On your wedding day make

sure you ____ and don't forget to _____ !!! To keep
(verb)   (verb)

a happy marriage, never, ever fight about _____.
(noun)

_____ and _____ and tell each other _____
(noun)   (noun)   (a phrase)

daily. I wish you lots of _____ and _____
(noun)   (noun)

for many years to come!

With Love, _____
(your name)

♥♥♥♥♥♥♥♥♥♥♥♥♥

Advice for the Bride-to-be

♥ ♡ ♥ ♡ ♥ ♡ ♥ ♡ ♥ ♡ ♥ ♡ ♥

Dear _____ (Bride's name)

I am so _____ that you are getting hitched! You
                (Adjective)

and _____ make such a _____ couple. I _____
      (Groom's name)   (Adjective)   (verb)

all the way from _____ to celebrate with you
                      (place)

today. Without any doubt you will be the most _____
                                                    (Adjective)

spouse because of your unique ability to _____ .
                                              (verb)

As your friend of _____ years, I will leave you with
                      (number)

a little bit of wisdom. On your wedding day make

sure you _____ and don't forget to _____ !!! To keep
              (verb)   (verb)

a happy marriage, never, ever fight about_____ .
                                                  (noun)

_____ and _____ and tell each other _____
  (noun)   (noun)   (a phrase)

daily. I wish you lots of_____ and _____
                              (noun)   (noun)

for many years to come!

With Love, _____
                    (your name)

♥ ♡ ♥ ♡ ♥ ♡ ♥ ♡ ♥ ♡ ♥ ♡ ♥

Advice for the *Bride-to-be*

♥ ♡ ♥ ♡ ♥ ♡ ♥ ♡ ♥ ♡ ♥ ♡ ♥

Dear _____ (Bride's name)

I am so _____ that you are getting hitched! You

and _____ make such a _____ couple. I _____
 (Groom's name)   (Adjective)   (verb)

all the way from _____ to celebrate with you
                      (place)

today. Without any doubt you will be the most _____
                                                 (Adjective)

spouse because of your unique ability to _____ .
                                           (verb)

As your friend of _____ years, I will leave you with
                   (number)

a little bit of wisdom. On your wedding day make

sure you _____ and don't forget to _____ !!! To keep
          (verb)   (verb)

a happy marriage, never, ever fight about _____ .
                                            (noun)

_____ and _____ and tell each other _____
 (noun)   (noun)   (a phrase)

daily. I wish you lots of _____ and _____
                           (noun)   (noun)

for many years to come!

With Love, _____
                (your name)

♥ ♡ ♥ ♡ ♥ ♡ ♥ ♡ ♥ ♡ ♥ ♡ ♥

Advice for the Bride-to-be

♥♥♥♥♥♥♥♥♥♥♥♥♥♥

Dear _____ (Bride's name)

I am so _____ that you are getting hitched! You
(Adjective)

and _____ make such a _____ couple. I _____
(Groom's name)   (Adjective)   (verb)

all the way from _____ to celebrate with you
(place)

today. Without any doubt you will be the most _____
(Adjective)

spouse because of your unique ability to _____ .
(verb)

As your friend of _____ years, I will leave you with
(number)

a little bit of wisdom. On your wedding day make

sure you _____ and don't forget to _____ !!! To keep
(verb)   (verb)

a happy marriage, never, ever fight about_____ .
(noun)

_____ and _____ and tell each other _____
(noun)   (noun)   (a phrase)

daily. I wish you lots of_____ and _____
(noun)   (noun)

for many years to come!

With Love, _____
(your name)

♥♥♥♥♥♥♥♥♥♥♥♥♥♥

Advice for the Bride-to-be

♥♥♥♥♥♥♥♥♥♥♥♥♥♥

Dear _____ (Bride's name)

I am so _____ that you are getting hitched! You
          (Adjective)

and _____ make such a _____ couple. I _____
    (Groom's name)   (Adjective)   (verb)

all the way from _____ to celebrate with you
                  (place)

today. Without any doubt you will be the most _____
                                              (Adjective)

spouse because of your unique ability to _____ .
                                          (verb)

As your friend of _____ years, I will leave you with
                  (number)

a little bit of wisdom. On your wedding day make

sure you _____ and don't forget to _____ !!! To keep
         (verb)   (verb)

a happy marriage, never, ever fight about_____ .
                                           (noun)

_____ and _____ and tell each other _____
(noun)   (noun)   (a phrase)

daily. I wish you lots of_____ and _____
                         (noun)   (noun)

for many years to come!

With Love, _____
                    (your name)

♥♥♥♥♥♥♥♥♥♥♥♥♥♥

Advice for the Bride-to-be

♥♥♥♥♥♥♥♥♥♥♥♥♥♥♥

Dear _____ (Bride's name)

I am so _____ that you are getting hitched! You
           (Adjective)

and _____ make such a _____ couple. I _____
      (Groom's name)   (Adjective)   (verb)

all the way from _____ to celebrate with you
                       (place)

today. Without any doubt you will be the most _____
                                                        (Adjective)

spouse because of your unique ability to _____ .
                                                (verb)

As your friend of _____ years, I will leave you with
                      (number)

a little bit of wisdom. On your wedding day make

sure you _____ and don't forget to _____!!! To keep
            (verb)   (verb)

a happy marriage, never, ever fight about_____ .
                                                   (noun)

_____ and _____ and tell each other _____
  (noun)   (noun)   (a phrase)

daily. I wish you lots of_____ and _____
                               (noun)   (noun)

for many years to come!

With Love, _____
                      (your name)

♥♥♥♥♥♥♥♥♥♥♥♥♥♥♥

Advice for the Bride-to-be

♥ ♥ ♥ ♥ ♥ ♥ ♥ ♥ ♥ ♥ ♥ ♥ ♥

Dear _____ (Bride's name)

I am so _____ that you are getting hitched! You

and _____ make such a _____ couple. I _____
(Groom's name)   (Adjective)   (verb)

all the way from _____ to celebrate with you
(place)

today. Without any doubt you will be the most _____
(Adjective)

spouse because of your unique ability to _____ .
(verb)

As your friend of _____ years, I will leave you with
(number)

a little bit of wisdom. On your wedding day make

sure you _____ and don't forget to _____ !!! To keep
(verb)   (verb)

a happy marriage, never, ever fight about _____ ,
(noun)

_____ and _____ and tell each other _____
(noun)   (noun)   (a phrase)

daily. I wish you lots of _____ and _____
(noun)   (noun)

for many years to come!

With Love, _____

(your name)

♥ ♥ ♥ ♥ ♥ ♥ ♥ ♥ ♥ ♥ ♥ ♥ ♥

Advice for the *Bride-to-be*

♥♡♥♡♥♡♥♡♥♡♥♡♥

Dear _____ (Bride's name)

I am so _____ that you are getting hitched! You
        (Adjective)

and _____ make such a _____ couple. I _____
     (Groom's name)   (Adjective)   (verb)

all the way from _____ to celebrate with you
                    (place)

today. Without any doubt you will be the most _____
                                                    (Adjective)

spouse because of your unique ability to _____ .
                                              (verb)

As your friend of _____ years, I will leave you with
                    (number)

a little bit of wisdom. On your wedding day make

sure you _____ and don't forget to _____ !!! To keep
          (verb)   (verb)

a happy marriage, never, ever fight about_____ .
                                               (noun)

_____ and _____ and tell each other _____
 (noun)   (noun)   (a phrase)

daily. I wish you lots of_____ and _____
                            (noun)   (noun)

for many years to come!

With Love, _____
                    (your name)

♥♡♥♡♥♡♥♡♥♡♥♡♥

Advice for the Bride-to-be

♥♡♥♡♥♡♥♡♥♡♥♡♥

Dear _____ (Bride's name)

I am so _____ that you are getting hitched! You
and _____ make such a _____ couple. I _____
(Groom's name)   (Adjective)   (verb)
all the way from _____ to celebrate with you
                 (place)
today. Without any doubt you will be the most ____
                                              (Adjective)
spouse because of your unique ability to _____ .
                                        (verb)
As your friend of ____ years, I will leave you with
                  (number)
a little bit of wisdom. On your wedding day make
sure you ____ and don't forget to ____ !!! To keep
        (verb)   (verb)
a happy marriage, never, ever fight about_____ ,
                                          (noun)
_____ and _____ and tell each other _____
(noun)   (noun)   (a phrase)
daily. I wish you lots of _____ and _____
                         (noun)   (noun)
for many years to come!

With Love, _____

                  (your name)

♥♡♥♡♥♡♥♡♥♡♥♡♥

Advice for the Bride-to-be

♥♥♥♥♥♥♥♥♥♥♥♥♥

Dear _____ (Bride's name)
I am so _____ that you are getting hitched! You
(Adjective)
and _____ make such a _____ couple. I _____
(Groom's name)   (Adjective)   (verb)
all the way from _____ to celebrate with you
(place)
today. Without any doubt you will be the most _____
(Adjective)
spouse because of your unique ability to _____.
(verb)
As your friend of _____ years, I will leave you with
(number)
a little bit of wisdom. On your wedding day make
sure you _____ and don't forget to _____ !!! To keep
(verb)   (verb)
a happy marriage, never, ever fight about _____.
(noun)
_____ and _____ and tell each other _____
(noun)   (noun)   (a phrase)
daily. I wish you lots of _____ and _____
(noun)   (noun)
for many years to come!

With Love, _____
(your name)

Advice for the Bride-to-be

♥♥♥♥♥♥♥♥♥♥♥♥♥♥♥

Dear _____ (Bride's name)

I am so _____ that you are getting hitched! You
and _____ make such a _____ couple. I _____
     (Groom's name)   (Adjective)   (verb)
all the way from _____ to celebrate with you
                    (place)
today. Without any doubt you will be the most _____
                                                  (Adjective)
spouse because of your unique ability to _____ .
                                            (verb)
As your friend of _____ years, I will leave you with
                    (number)
a little bit of wisdom. On your wedding day make
sure you _____ and don't forget to _____ !!! To keep
           (verb)   (verb)
a happy marriage, never, ever fight about_____ .
                                             (noun)
_____ and _____ and tell each other_____
 (noun)   (noun)   (a phrase)
daily. I wish you lots of_____ and _____
                          (noun)   (noun)
for many years to come!

With Love, _____
                    (your name)

♥♥♥♥♥♥♥♥♥♥♥♥♥♥♥

Advice for the *Bride-to-be*

♥♡♥♡♥♡♥♡♥♡♥♡♥

Dear _____ (Bride's name)

I am so _____ that you are getting hitched! You
(Adjective)

and _____ make such a _____ couple. I _____
(Groom's name)   (Adjective)   (verb)

all the way from _____ to celebrate with you
(place)

today. Without any doubt you will be the most _____
(Adjective)

spouse because of your unique ability to _____ .
(verb)

As your friend of _____ years, I will leave you with
(number)

a little bit of wisdom. On your wedding day make

sure you ____ and don't forget to _____ !!! To keep
(verb)   (verb)

a happy marriage, never, ever fight about _____ .
(noun)

_____ and _____ and tell each other _____
(noun)   (noun)   (a phrase)

daily. I wish you lots of _____ and _____
(noun)   (noun)

for many years to come!

With Love, _____
(your name)

Advice for the Bride-to-be

♥ ♡ ♥ ♡ ♥ ♡ ♥ ♡ ♥ ♡ ♥ ♡ ♥

Dear _____ (Bride's name)

I am so _____ that you are getting hitched! You
(Adjective)
and _____ make such a _____ couple. I _____
(Groom's name)   (Adjective)   (verb)
all the way from _____ to celebrate with you
(place)
today. Without any doubt you will be the most _____
(Adjective)
spouse because of your unique ability to _____ .
(verb)
As your friend of _____ years, I will leave you with
(number)
a little bit of wisdom. On your wedding day make
sure you ____ and don't forget to _____ !!! To keep
(verb)   (verb)
a happy marriage, never, ever fight about_____ ,
(noun)
_____ and _____ and tell each other _____
(noun)   (noun)   (a phrase)
daily. I wish you lots of _____ and _____
(noun)   (noun)
for many years to come!

With Love, _____
(your name)

♥ ♡ ♥ ♡ ♥ ♡ ♥ ♡ ♥ ♡ ♥ ♡ ♥

Advice for the Bride-to-be

♥ ♡ ♥ ♡ ♥ ♡ ♥ ♡ ♥ ♡ ♥ ♡ ♥

Dear _____ (Bride's name)

I am so _____ that you are getting hitched! You
(Adjective)

and _____ make such a _____ couple. I _____
(Groom's name) _(Adjective)_ _(verb)_

all the way from _____ to celebrate with you
(place)

today. Without any doubt you will be the most _____
(Adjective)

spouse because of your unique ability to _____ .
(verb)

As your friend of _____ years, I will leave you with
(number)

a little bit of wisdom. On your wedding day make

sure you _____ and don't forget to _____ !!! To keep
(verb) _(verb)_

a happy marriage, never, ever fight about _____ .
(noun)

_____ and _____ and tell each other _____
(noun) _(noun)_ _(a phrase)_

daily. I wish you lots of _____ and _____
(noun) _(noun)_

for many years to come!

With Love, _____
(your name)

♥ ♡ ♥ ♡ ♥ ♡ ♥ ♡ ♥ ♡ ♥ ♡ ♥

Advice for the Bride-to-be

♥♥♥♥♥♥♥♥♥♥♥♥♥♥

Dear _____ (Bride's name)

I am so _____ that you are getting hitched! You

(Adjective)

and _____ make such a _____ couple. I _____

(Groom's name)   (Adjective)   (verb)

all the way from _____ to celebrate with you

(place)

today. Without any doubt you will be the most _____

(Adjective)

spouse because of your unique ability to _____ .

(verb)

As your friend of _____ years, I will leave you with

(number)

a little bit of wisdom. On your wedding day make

sure you ____ and don't forget to _____ !!! To keep

(verb)   (verb)

a happy marriage, never, ever fight about_____ .

(noun)

_____ and _____ and tell each other_____

(noun)   (noun)   (a phrase)

daily. I wish you lots of_____ and _____

(noun)   (noun)

for many years to come!

With Love, _____

(your name)

♥♥♥♥♥♥♥♥♥♥♥♥♥♥

Advice for the *Bride-to-be*

♥♡♥♡♥♡♥♡♥♡♥♡♥

Dear _____ (Bride's name)

I am so _____ that you are getting hitched! You
       (Adjective)

and _____ make such a _____ couple. I _____
   (Groom's name)   (Adjective)   (verb)

all the way from _____ to celebrate with you
                  (place)

today. Without any doubt you will be the most _____
                                               (Adjective)

spouse because of your unique ability to _____ .
                                          (verb)

As your friend of _____ years, I will leave you with
                   (number)

a little bit of wisdom. On your wedding day make

sure you _____ and don't forget to _____ !!! To keep
         (verb)   (verb)

a happy marriage, never, ever fight about_____ .
                                           (noun)

_____ and _____ and tell each other _____
(noun)   (noun)   (a phrase)

daily. I wish you lots of_____ and _____
                          (noun)   (noun)

for many years to come!

With Love, _____
            (your name)

Advice for the Bride-to-be

♥ ♥ ♥ ♥ ♥ ♥ ♥ ♥ ♥ ♥ ♥ ♥ ♥

Dear _____ (Bride's name)

I am so _____ that you are getting hitched! You
(Adjective)

and _____ make such a _____ couple. I _____
(Groom's name)   (Adjective)   (verb)

all the way from _____ to celebrate with you
(place)

today. Without any doubt you will be the most _____
(Adjective)

spouse because of your unique ability to _____ .
(verb)

As your friend of _____ years, I will leave you with
(number)

a little bit of wisdom. On your wedding day make

sure you _____ and don't forget to _____ !!! To keep
(verb)   (verb)

a happy marriage, never, ever fight about _____ ,
(noun)

_____ and _____ and tell each other _____
(noun)   (noun)   (a phrase)

daily. I wish you lots of _____ and _____
(noun)   (noun)

for many years to come!

With Love, _____
(your name)

Advice for the Bride-to-be

♥ ♥ ♥ ♥ ♥ ♥ ♥ ♥ ♥ ♥ ♥ ♥ ♥ ♥

Dear _____ (Bride's name)

I am so _____ that you are getting hitched! You
(Adjective)

and _____ make such a _____ couple. I _____
(Groom's name)   (Adjective)   (verb)

all the way from _____ to celebrate with you
(place)

today. Without any doubt you will be the most _____
(Adjective)

spouse because of your unique ability to _____ .
(verb)

As your friend of _____ years, I will leave you with
(number)

a little bit of wisdom. On your wedding day make

sure you _____ and don't forget to _____ !!! To keep
(verb)   (verb)

a happy marriage, never, ever fight about_____ .
(noun)

_____ and _____ and tell each other_____
(noun)   (noun)   (a phrase)

daily. I wish you lots of_____ and _____
(noun)   (noun)

for many years to come!

With Love, _____
(your name)

♥ ♥ ♥ ♥ ♥ ♥ ♥ ♥ ♥ ♥ ♥ ♥ ♥ ♥

Advice for the Bride-to-be

♥ ♡ ♥ ♡ ♥ ♡ ♥ ♡ ♥ ♡ ♥ ♡ ♥

Dear _____ (Bride's name)

I am so _____ that you are getting hitched! You
(Adjective)

and _____ make such a _____ couple. I _____
(Groom's name)   (Adjective)   (verb)

all the way from _____ to celebrate with you
(place)

today. Without any doubt you will be the most _____
(Adjective)

spouse because of your unique ability to _____ .
(verb)

As your friend of _____ years, I will leave you with
(number)

a little bit of wisdom. On your wedding day make

sure you _____ and don't forget to _____ !!! To keep
(verb)   (verb)

a happy marriage, never, ever fight about _____ .
(noun)

_____ and _____ and tell each other _____
(noun)   (noun)   (a phrase)

daily. I wish you lots of _____ and _____
(noun)   (noun)

for many years to come!

With Love, _____
(your name)

♥ ♡ ♥ ♡ ♥ ♡ ♥ ♡ ♥ ♡ ♥ ♡ ♥

Advice for the Bride-to-be

♥♡♥♡♥♡♥♡♥♡♥♡♥

Dear _____ (Bride's name)

I am so _____ that you are getting hitched! You
(Adjective)

and _____ make such a _____ couple. I _____
(Groom's name)   (Adjective)   (verb)

all the way from _____ to celebrate with you
(place)

today. Without any doubt you will be the most _____
(Adjective)

spouse because of your unique ability to _____ .
(verb)

As your friend of _____ years, I will leave you with
(number)

a little bit of wisdom. On your wedding day make

sure you _____ and don't forget to _____ !!! To keep
(verb)   (verb)

a happy marriage, never, ever fight about _____ .
(noun)

_____ and _____ and tell each other _____
(noun)   (noun)   (a phrase)

daily. I wish you lots of _____ and _____
(noun)   (noun)

for many years to come!

With Love, _____
(your name)

Advice for the *Bride-to-be*

♥♡♥♡♥♡♥♡♥♡♥♡♥♡♥

Dear _____ (Bride's name)

I am so _____ that you are getting hitched! You
and _____ make such a _____ couple. I _____
(Groom's name) _____ (Adjective) _____ (verb)
all the way from _____ to celebrate with you
(place)
today. Without any doubt you will be the most _____
(Adjective)
spouse because of your unique ability to _____.
(verb)
As your friend of ____ years, I will leave you with
(number)
a little bit of wisdom. On your wedding day make
sure you ____ and don't forget to _____!!! To keep
(verb) (verb)
a happy marriage, never, ever fight about_____.
(noun)
_____ and _____ and tell each other_____
(noun) (noun) (a phrase)
daily. I wish you lots of_____ and _____
(noun) (noun)
for many years to come!

With Love, _____
(your name)

Advice for the Bride-to-be

♥♡♥♡♥♡♥♡♥♡♥♡♥

Dear _____ (Bride's name)

I am so _____ that you are getting hitched! You
(Adjective)

and _____ make such a _____ couple. I _____
(Groom's name)   (Adjective)   (verb)

all the way from _____ to celebrate with you
(place)

today. Without any doubt you will be the most _____
(Adjective)

spouse because of your unique ability to _____ .
(verb)

As your friend of _____ years, I will leave you with
(number)

a little bit of wisdom. On your wedding day make

sure you _____ and don't forget to _____ !!! To keep
(verb)   (verb)

a happy marriage, never, ever fight about_____ .
(noun)

_____ and _____ and tell each other _____
(noun)   (noun)   (a phrase)

daily. I wish you lots of_____ and _____
(noun)   (noun)

for many years to come!

With Love, _____
(your name)

Advice for the Bride-to-be

♥♡♥♡♥♡♥♡♥♡♥♡♥

Dear _____ (Bride's name)

I am so _____ that you are getting hitched! You
    (Adjective)

and _____ make such a _____ couple. I _____
    (Groom's name)   (Adjective)   (verb)

all the way from _____ to celebrate with you
                    (place)

today. Without any doubt you will be the most _____
                                                  (Adjective)

spouse because of your unique ability to _____ .
                                            (verb)

As your friend of _____ years, I will leave you with
                    (number)

a little bit of wisdom. On your wedding day make

sure you _____ and don't forget to _____ !!! To keep
          (verb)   (verb)

a happy marriage, never, ever fight about _____ .
                                              (noun)

_____ and _____ and tell each other _____
(noun)   (noun)   (a phrase)

daily. I wish you lots of _____ and _____
                             (noun)   (noun)

for many years to come!

With Love, _____
              (your name)

♥♡♥♡♥♡♥♡♥♡♥♡♥

Advice for the Bride-to-be

♥♡♥♡♥♡♥♡♥♡♥

Dear _____ (Bride's name)

I am so _____ that you are getting hitched! You
(Adjective)

and _____ make such a _____ couple. I _____
(Groom's name)   (Adjective)   (verb)

all the way from _____ to celebrate with you
(place)

today. Without any doubt you will be the most _____
(Adjective)

spouse because of your unique ability to _____ .
(verb)

As your friend of _____ years, I will leave you with
(number)

a little bit of wisdom. On your wedding day make

sure you _____ and don't forget to _____ !!!! To keep
(verb)   (verb)

a happy marriage, never, ever fight about _____ ,
(noun)

_____ and _____ and tell each other _____
(noun)   (noun)   (a phrase)

daily. I wish you lots of _____ and _____
(noun)   (noun)

for many years to come!

With Love, _____
(your name)

♥♡♥♡♥♡♥♡♥♡♥

Advice for the Bride-to-be

♥ ♡ ♥ ♡ ♥ ♡ ♥ ♡ ♥ ♡ ♥ ♡ ♥

Dear _____ (Bride's name)

I am so _____ that you are getting hitched! You
(Adjective)

and _____ make such a _____ couple. I _____
(Groom's name)   (Adjective)   (verb)

all the way from _____ to celebrate with you
(place)

today. Without any doubt you will be the most _____
(Adjective)

spouse because of your unique ability to _____ .
(verb)

As your friend of _____ years, I will leave you with
(number)

a little bit of wisdom. On your wedding day make

sure you ____ and don't forget to _____!!! To keep
(verb)   (verb)

a happy marriage, never, ever fight about _____ .
(noun)

_____ and _____ and tell each other _____
(noun)   (noun)   (a phrase)

daily. I wish you lots of _____ and _____
(noun)   (noun)

for many years to come!

With Love, _____
(your name)

♥ ♡ ♥ ♡ ♥ ♡ ♥ ♡ ♥ ♡ ♥ ♡ ♥

Advice for the Bride-to-be

♥♥♥♥♥♥♥♥♥♥♥♥♥♥♥

Dear _____ (Bride's name)

I am so _____ that you are getting hitched! You
and _____ make such a _____ couple. I _____
    (Groom's name)   (Adjective)   couple. I _____
                                                              (verb)
all the way from _____ to celebrate with you
                  (place)
today. Without any doubt you will be the most _____
                                               (Adjective)
spouse because of your unique ability to _____ .
                                          (verb)
As your friend of _____ years, I will leave you with
                  (number)
a little bit of wisdom. On your wedding day make
sure you _____ and don't forget to _____!!! To keep
         (verb)   (verb)
a happy marriage, never, ever fight about_____ ,
                                        (noun)
_____ and _____ and tell each other_____
(noun)   (noun)   (a phrase)
daily. I wish you lots of_____ and _____
                         (noun)   (noun)
for many years to come!

With Love, _____
              (your name)

♥♥♥♥♥♥♥♥♥♥♥♥♥♥♥

Advice for the Bride-to-be

Dear _____ (Bride's name)

I am so _____ that you are getting hitched! You and _____ make such a _____ couple. I _____ all the way from _____ to celebrate with you today. Without any doubt you will be the most ____ spouse because of your unique ability to _____ .

(Adjective) (Groom's name) (Adjective) (verb) (place) (Adjective) (verb)

As your friend of ____ years, I will leave you with a little bit of wisdom. On your wedding day make sure you ____ and don't forget to _____ !!! To keep a happy marriage, never, ever fight about_____ . _____ and _____ and tell each other_____ daily. I wish you lots of_____ and _____ for many years to come!

(number) (verb) (verb) (noun) (noun) (noun) (a phrase) (noun) (noun)

With Love, _____

(your name)

Advice for the Bride-to-be

♥ ♡ ♥ ♡ ♥ ♡ ♥ ♡ ♥ ♡ ♥

Dear _____ (Bride's name)

I am so _____ that you are getting hitched! You
          (Adjective)
and _____ make such a _____ couple. I _____
     (Groom's name)   (Adjective)   (verb)
all the way from _____ to celebrate with you
                    (place)
today. Without any doubt you will be the most _____
                                                (Adjective)
spouse because of your unique ability to _____ .
                                          (verb)
As your friend of _____ years, I will leave you with
                  (number)
a little bit of wisdom. On your wedding day make
sure you _____ and don't forget to _____ !!! To keep
          (verb)   (verb)
a happy marriage, never, ever fight about _____ ,
                                           (noun)
_____ and _____ and tell each other _____
(noun)   (noun)   (a phrase)
daily. I wish you lots of _____ and _____
                          (noun)   (noun)
for many years to come!

With Love, _____
                (your name)

Advice for the Bride-to-be

♥♡♥♡♥♡♥♡♥♡♥♡♥♡♥♡♥

Dear _____ (Bride's name)

I am so _____ that you are getting hitched! You
(Adjective)

and _____ make such a _____ couple. I _____
(Groom's name)   (Adjective)   (verb)

all the way from _____ to celebrate with you
(place)

today. Without any doubt you will be the most ____
(Adjective)

spouse because of your unique ability to _____ .
(verb)

As your friend of ____ years, I will leave you with
(number)

a little bit of wisdom. On your wedding day make

sure you ____ and don't forget to _____ !!! To keep
(verb)   (verb)

a happy marriage, never, ever fight about _____ .
(noun)

_____ and _____ and tell each other _____
(noun)   (noun)   (a phrase)

daily. I wish you lots of _____ and _____
(noun)   (noun)

for many years to come!

With Love, _____
(your name)

Advice for the Bride-to-Be

♥♥♥♥♥♥♥♥♥♥♥♥

Dear _____ (Bride's name)

I am so _____ that you are getting hitched! You
(Adjective)

and _____ make such a _____ couple. I _____
(Groom's name)   (Adjective)   (verb)

all the way from _____ to celebrate with you
(place)

today. Without any doubt you will be the most ____
(Adjective)

spouse because of your unique ability to _____ .
(verb)

As your friend of ____ years, I will leave you with
(Number)

a little bit of wisdom. On your wedding day make

sure you ____ and don't forget to _____ !!! To keep
(verb)   (verb)

a happy marriage, never, ever fight about _____ ,
(noun)

_____ and _____ and tell each other _____
(noun)   (noun)   (a phrase)

daily. I wish you lots of _____ and _____
(noun)   (noun)

for many years to come!

With Love, _____
(your name)

♥♥♥♥♥♥♥♥♥♥♥♥

Advice for the Bride-to-be

♥♡♥♡♥♡♥♡♥♡♥♡♥♡♥

Dear _____ (Bride's name)

I am so _____that you are getting hitched! You
    (Adjective)
and _____make such a _____ couple. I _____
   (Groom's name)   (Adjective)   (verb)
all the way from _____ to celebrate with you
               (place)
today. Without any doubt you will be the most _____
                                            (Adjective)
spouse because of your unique ability to _____.
                                      (verb)
As your friend of_____years, I will leave you with
              (number)
a little bit of wisdom. On your wedding day make
sure you____ and don't forget to _____!!! To keep
      (verb)   (verb)
a happy marriage, never, ever fight about_____,
                                      (noun)
_____ and _____ and tell each other_____
(noun)   (noun)   (a phrase)
daily. I wish you lots of_____ and _____
                      (noun)   (noun)
for many years to come!

With Love, _____
                  (your name)

♥♡♥♡♥♡♥♡♥♡♥♡♥♡♥

Advice for the Bride-to-be

♥♥♥♥♥♥♥♥♥♥♥♥♥

Dear _____ (Bride's name)

I am so _____ that you are getting hitched! You
(Adjective)

and _____ make such a _____ couple. I _____
(Groom's name)   (Adjective)   (verb)

all the way from _____ to celebrate with you
(place)

today. Without any doubt you will be the most _____
(Adjective)

spouse because of your unique ability to _____ .
(verb)

As your friend of _____ years, I will leave you with
(number)

a little bit of wisdom. On your wedding day make

sure you _____ and don't forget to _____ !!!! To keep
(verb)   (verb)

a happy marriage, never, ever fight about _____ .
(noun)

_____ and _____ and tell each other _____
(noun)   (noun)   (a phrase)

daily. I wish you lots of _____ and _____
(noun)   (noun)

for many years to come!

With Love, _____
(your name)

Advice for the Bride-to-be

♥♥♥♥♥♥♥♥♥♥♥♥♥

Dear _____ (Bride's name)

I am so _____ that you are getting hitched! You and _____ make such a _____ couple. I _____
(Groom's name)   (Adjective)   (verb)

all the way from _____ to celebrate with you
(place)

today. Without any doubt you will be the most _____
(Adjectiv

spouse because of your unique ability to _____ .
(verb)

As your friend of _____ years, I will leave you with
(number)

a little bit of wisdom. On your wedding day make

sure you _____ and don't forget to _____ !!! To keep
(verb)   (verb)

a happy marriage, never, ever fight about _____ ,
(noun)

_____ and _____ and tell each other _____
(noun)   (noun)   (a phrase)

daily. I wish you lots of _____ and _____
(noun)   (noun)

for many years to come!

With Love, _____
(your name)

Advice for the *Bride-to-be*

♥ ♡ ♥ ♡ ♥ ♡ ♥ ♡ ♥ ♡ ♥ ♡ ♥

Dear _____ (Bride's name)

I am so _____ that you are getting hitched! You
(Adjective)

and _____ make such a _____ couple. I _____
(Groom's name)   (Adjective)   (verb)

all the way from _____ to celebrate with you
(place)

today. Without any doubt you will be the most _____
(Adjective)

spouse because of your unique ability to _____ .
(verb)

As your friend of _____ years, I will leave you with
(number)

a little bit of wisdom. On your wedding day make

sure you _____ and don't forget to _____ !!!! To keep
(verb)   (verb)

a happy marriage, never, ever fight about_____ .
(noun)

_____ and _____ and tell each other_____
(noun)   (noun)   (a phrase)

daily. I wish you lots of_____ and _____
(noun)   (noun)

for many years to come!

With Love, _____
(your name)

Advice for the Bride-to-be

Dear _____ (Bride's name)

I am so _____ that you are getting hitched! You
and _____ make such a _____ couple. I _____
(Groom's name)   (Adjective)   (verb)
all the way from _____ to celebrate with you
(place)
today. Without any doubt you will be the most _____
(Adjective)
spouse because of your unique ability to _____ .
(verb)
As your friend of _____ years, I will leave you with
(number)
a little bit of wisdom. On your wedding day make
sure you ____ and don't forget to _____ !!! To keep
(verb)   (verb)
a happy marriage, never, ever fight about _____ .
(noun)
_____ and _____ and tell each other _____
(noun)   (noun)   (a phrase)
daily. I wish you lots of _____ and _____
(noun)   (noun)
for many years to come!

With Love, _____
(your name)

Advice for the *Bride-to-be*

♥♡♥♡♥♡♥♡♥♡♥♡♥♡♥

Dear _____ (Bride's name)

I am so _____ that you are getting hitched! You
            (Adjective)

and _____ make such a _____ couple. I _____
    (Groom's name)   (Adjective)   (verb)

all the way from _____ to celebrate with you
                    (place)

today. Without any doubt you will be the most _____
                                              (Adjective)

spouse because of your unique ability to _____ .
                                          (verb)

As your friend of _____ years, I will leave you with
                  (number)

a little bit of wisdom. On your wedding day make

sure you _____ and don't forget to _____ !!! To keep
         (verb)   (verb)

a happy marriage, never, ever fight about _____ .
                                          (noun)

_____ and _____ and tell each other _____
(noun)   (noun)   (a phrase)

daily. I wish you lots of _____ and _____
                          (noun)   (noun)

for many years to come!

With Love, _____

(your name)

♥♡♥♡♥♡♥♡♥♡♥♡♥♡♥

Advice for the Bride-to-be

♥♥♥♥♥♥♥♥♥♥♥♥♥♥♥

Dear _____ (Bride's name)

I am so _____ that you are getting hitched! You
   (Adjective)

and _____ make such a _____ couple. I _____
   (Groom's name)   (Adjective)   (verb)

all the way from _____ to celebrate with you
                    (place)

today. Without any doubt you will be the most _____
                                               (Adjective)

spouse because of your unique ability to _____ .
                                            (verb)

As your friend of _____ years, I will leave you with
                   (number)

a little bit of wisdom. On your wedding day make

sure you _____ and don't forget to _____!!! To keep
          (verb)   (verb)

a happy marriage, never, ever fight about _____ .
                                            (noun)

_____ and _____ and tell each other _____
 (noun)   (noun)   (a phrase)

daily. I wish you lots of _____ and _____
                           (noun)   (noun)

for many years to come!

With Love, _____
                  (your name)

Advice for the Bride-to-be

♥♥♥♥♥♥♥♥♥♥♥♥♥♥

Dear _____ (Bride's name)

I am so _____ that you are getting hitched! You

and _____ make such a _____ couple. I _____
   (Groom's name)   (Adjective)   (verb)

all the way from _____ to celebrate with you
                  (place)

today. Without any doubt you will be the most _____
                                              (Adjective)

spouse because of your unique ability to _____ .
                                          (verb)

As your friend of _____ years, I will leave you with
                  (number)

a little bit of wisdom. On your wedding day make

sure you _____ and don't forget to _____ !!!! To keep
         (verb)   (verb)

a happy marriage, never, ever fight about_____ .
                                          (noun)

_____ and _____ and tell each other _____
(noun)   (noun)   (a phrase)

daily. I wish you lots of _____ and _____
                          (noun)   (noun)

for many years to come!

With Love, _____
              (your name)

Advice for the *Bride-to-be*

♥♡♥♡♥♡♥♡♥♡♥♡♥♡♥♡♥

Dear _____ (Bride's name)

I am so _____ that you are getting hitched! You
(Adjective)

and _____ make such a _____ couple. I _____
(Groom's name)   (Adjective)   (verb)

all the way from _____ to celebrate with you
(place)

today. Without any doubt you will be the most _____
(Adjective)

spouse because of your unique ability to _____ .
(verb)

As your friend of _____ years, I will leave you with
(number)

a little bit of wisdom. On your wedding day make

sure you ____ and don't forget to _____ !!! To keep
(verb)   (verb)

a happy marriage, never, ever fight about _____ .
(noun)

_____ and _____ and tell each other _____
(noun)   (noun)   (a phrase)

daily. I wish you lots of _____ and _____
(noun)   (noun)

for many years to come!

With Love, _____
(your name)

Advice for the Bride-to-be

♥♥♥♥♥♥♥♥♥♥♥♥♥

Dear _____ (Bride's name)

I am so _____ that you are getting hitched! You
(Adjective)

and _____make such a _____ couple. I _____
(Groom's name)   (Adjective)   (verb)

all the way from _____ to celebrate with you
(place)

today. Without any doubt you will be the most _____
(Adjective)

spouse because of your unique ability to _____ .
(verb)

As your friend of ____ years, I will leave you with
(number)

a little bit of wisdom. On your wedding day make

sure you ____ and don't forget to _____ !!! To keep
(verb)   (verb)

a happy marriage, never, ever fight about_____ .
(noun)

_____ and _____ and tell each other_____
(noun)   (noun)   (a phrase)

daily. I wish you lots of_____ and _____
(noun)   (noun)

for many years to come!

With Love, _____
(your name)

Advice for the Bride-to-Be

♥♡♥♡♥♡♥♡♥♡♥

Dear _____ (Bride's name)

I am so _____ that you are getting hitched! You
          (Adjective)

and _____ make such a _____ couple. I _____
    (Groom's name)   (Adjective)   (verb)

all the way from _____ to celebrate with you
                 (place)

today. Without any doubt you will be the most _____
                                              (Adjecti...

spouse because of your unique ability to _____ .
                                         (verb)

As your friend of _____ years, I will leave you with
                  (Number)

a little bit of wisdom. On your wedding day make

sure you _____ and don't forget to _____!!! To keep
         (verb)   (verb)

a happy marriage, never, ever fight about _____ ,
                                          (noun)

_____ and _____ and tell each other _____
(noun)   (noun)   (a phrase)

daily. I wish you lots of _____ and _____
                          (noun)   (noun)

for many years to come!

                    With Love, _____
                                (your name)

Advice for the Bride-to-be

♥♥♥♥♥♥♥♥♥♥♥♥♥♥♥

Dear _____ (Bride's name)

I am so _____ that you are getting hitched! You
(Adjective)

and _____ make such a _____ couple. I _____
(Groom's name)   (Adjective)   (verb)

all the way from _____ to celebrate with you
(place)

today. Without any doubt you will be the most _____
(Adjective)

spouse because of your unique ability to _____ .
(verb)

As your friend of _____ years, I will leave you with
(number)

a little bit of wisdom. On your wedding day make

sure you _____ and don't forget to _____ !!! To keep
(verb)   (verb)

a happy marriage, never, ever fight about _____ .
(noun)

_____ and _____ and tell each other _____
(noun)   (noun)   (a phrase)

daily. I wish you lots of _____ and _____
(noun)   (noun)

for many years to come!

With Love, _____
(your name)

Advice for the Bride-to-be

♥♡♥♡♥♡♥♡♥♡♥♡♥

Dear _____ (Bride's name)
I am so _____ that you are getting hitched! You
(Adjective)
and _____ make such a _____ couple. I _____
(Groom's name)   (Adjective)   (verb)
all the way from _____ to celebrate with you
(place)
today. Without any doubt you will be the most _____
(Adjectiv
spouse because of your unique ability to _____ .
(verb)
As your friend of _____ years, I will leave you with
(number)
a little bit of wisdom. On your wedding day make
sure you _____ and don't forget to _____!!! To keep
(verb)   (verb)
a happy marriage, never, ever fight about_____ .
(noun)
_____ and _____ and tell each other_____
(noun)   (noun)   (a phrase)
daily. I wish you lots of_____ and _____
(noun)   (noun)
for many years to come!

With Love, _____
(your name)

♥♡♥♡♥♡♥♡♥♡♥♡♥

Advice for the Bride-to-be

♥ ♥ ♥ ♥ ♥ ♥ ♥ ♥ ♥ ♥ ♥ ♥

Dear _____ (Bride's name)

I am so _____ (Adjective) that you are getting hitched! You

and _____ (Groom's name) make such a _____ (Adjective) couple. I _____ (verb)

all the way from _____ (place) to celebrate with you

today. Without any doubt you will be the most _____ (Adjective)

spouse because of your unique ability to _____ (verb) .

As your friend of _____ (number) years, I will leave you with

a little bit of wisdom. On your wedding day make

sure you _____ (verb) and don't forget to _____ (verb) !!! To keep

a happy marriage, never, ever fight about _____ (noun) ,

_____ (noun) and _____ (noun) and tell each other _____ (a phrase)

daily. I wish you lots of _____ (noun) and _____ (noun)

for many years to come!

With Love, _____ (your name)

Advice for the Bride-to-be

♥♡♥♡♥♡♥♡♥♡♥♡♥

Dear _____ (Bride's name)

I am so _____ that you are getting hitched! You
(Adjective)

and _____ make such a _____ couple. I _____
(Groom's name)   (Adjective)   (verb)

all the way from _____ to celebrate with you
(place)

today. Without any doubt you will be the most _____
(Adjective)

spouse because of your unique ability to _____ .
(verb)

As your friend of _____ years, I will leave you with
(number)

a little bit of wisdom. On your wedding day make

sure you _____ and don't forget to _____ !!! To keep
(verb)   (verb)

a happy marriage, never, ever fight about _____ .
(noun)

_____ and _____ and tell each other _____
(noun)   (noun)   (a phrase)

daily. I wish you lots of _____ and _____
(noun)   (noun)

for many years to come!

With Love, _____
(your name)

Advice for the Bride-to-be

♥♡♥♡♥♡♥♡♥♡♥♡♥

Dear _____ (Bride's name)
I am so _____ that you are getting hitched! You
(Adjective)
and _____ make such a _____ couple. I _____
(Groom's name) *(Adjective)* *(verb)*
all the way from _____ to celebrate with you
(place)
today. Without any doubt you will be the most ____
(Adjective)
spouse because of your unique ability to _____ .
(verb)
As your friend of ____ years, I will leave you with
(number)
a little bit of wisdom. On your wedding day make
sure you ____ and don't forget to ____ !!! To keep
(verb) *(verb)*
a happy marriage, never, ever fight about _____ .
(noun)
_____ and _____ and tell each other _____
(noun) *(noun)* *(a phrase)*
daily. I wish you lots of _____ and _____
(noun) *(noun)*
for many years to come!

With Love, _____
(your name)

♥♡♥♡♥♡♥♡♥♡♥♡♥

Made in United States
North Haven, CT
09 April 2022

18065822R00031

ISBN 9781078137454

9 781078 137454

90000